Disney · PIXAR

TOY STORY 3

P9-BAU-031

Hope you
love Toy Story
as much as
we do!
Love,
Pollit & Brenton
Elliott

Attic

Adapted by
Annie Auerbach

Illustrated by
Adrian Molina

Designed by
Tony Fejeran

 A GOLDEN BOOK • NEW YORK

Copyright © 2010 Disney/Pixar. All rights reserved. Slinky® Dog is a registered trademark of Poof-Slinky, Inc.
© Poof-Slinky, Inc. Published in the United States by Golden Books, an imprint of Random House Children's Books,
a division of Random House, Inc., 1745 Broadway, New York, NY 10019, and in Canada by Random House of
Canada Limited, Toronto, in conjunction with Disney Enterprises, Inc. Golden Books, A Golden Book,
the G colophon, and the distinctive gold spine are registered trademarks of Random House, Inc.

www.randomhouse.com/kids

Library of Congress Control Number: 2009933254

ISBN: 978-0-7364-2668-8

Printed in the United States of America

10 9 8 7

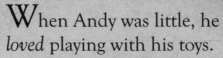

When Andy was little, he *loved* playing with his toys. There were **Rex, Hamm, Jessie, Bullseye, Buzz Lightyear, Slinky Dog, the Aliens** . . .

. . . and Andy's very favorite toy—**Sheriff Woody**.

Now Andy has **GROWN UP** and is packing for college. He is going to take Woody with him.

Andy plans to store his other toys in the attic.
But Andy's mom picks up the bag by mistake.
Oh, no! She thinks it's trash!

Luckily, the toys avoid the garbage truck. They make a daring **ESCAPE** to the garage!

Woody explains that it was a big mistake—Andy didn't mean to throw them away. But no one believes him.

Jessie spots a donation box, and the toys climb in.

The box of toys gets donated to Sunnyside Daycare. Jessie, Buzz, and the gang are thrilled! They find **cheerful toys** and all the **extra batteries** they could want!

Lots-o'-Huggin' Bear welcomes the new toys warmly. "Being donated was the best thing that ever happened to you!" says Lotso. "You'll never be outgrown or forgotten."

Woody still doesn't think they belong there. "We're *Andy's* toys," he says. He leaves for home by himself.

He uses a kite to go **UP**!

Then he goes **DOWN**!

A little girl named Bonnie finds Woody and takes him to her house.

Back at Sunnyside, things are not so sunny.
The daycare children **THROW**, **SMASH**,
and **SLOBBER ON** the toys.

Everyone feels **ACHY** and **HURT**. Woody was right—they don't belong here. The toys need help! They want to go back to Andy.

That night, Buzz goes to talk to Lotso.

But there is one more big problem. . . .

It's **Lotso**! He wants Andy's toys to stay with the toddlers who haven't learned to play nicely with toys yet. That's so the toddlers won't play with *him*!

Lotso gets his toughest friends to capture Buzz. The space ranger is in trouble!

The other toys are in trouble, too!
Lotso locks them in **jail** for the night . . .
and Buzz is the guard! Lotso has pressed a button
on Buzz. The space ranger now believes that
Andy's toys are **enemies** working for the evil
Emperor Zurg!

Meanwhile, Woody is having fun at Bonnie's house. He meets nice toys.

An old clown named Chuckles says that he knew Lotso a long time ago. Woody learns that Lotso is bad—and his friends are in **DANGER**!

Woody wants to go
home to Andy, but his
friends need
help!

Woody sneaks back
into Sunnyside. The
toys **PLAN** their escape.

Woody and Slinky
GRAB the daycare keys!

It's time to **RE/ET** Buzz.

The toys sneak
across the playground.
Shhh!

"This is the only
way out," says Woody.

Oh, no! Lotso is waiting at the Dumpster.

The toys struggle to get past Lotso. But a
garbage truck arrives. Now everyone is headed
for the **garbage dump**!

At the dump, the toys are **PUSHED** onto a conveyor belt. They're moving toward the **incinerator**! The toys are scared, but everyone sticks together.

The toys give Lotso a boost so he can reach the **STOP** button. But Lotso changes his mind . . . and *doesn't* push the button!

"NOOO!"

yells Woody as he and the other toys come closer to the fire.

Suddenly, a huge claw **SCOOPS** the toys up. The Aliens have saved their friends!

Lotso finds a new home . . .

COLLEGE

Attic

DONATE TO:
1225
SYCAMORE

. . . while the toys return to their old one.
But Woody knows that things will never
be like they used to be. Andy has grown up.
Then Woody has an **idea**.

At first, Andy isn't sure he wants to give away his toys. But when he meets Bonnie, he knows they will be
LOVED.

Woody and Buzz watch as Andy drives away.

"So long, partner," says Woody. Although Woody will miss his friend, Andy will always have a special place in his **heart**.